Puddin

by

Pearl Bancroft

pearl bancroft
Rita Schwarz

xulon PRESS

Puddin
by Pearl Bancroft

Printed in the United States of America

ISBN 978-1-60647-083-1

www.xulonpress.com

To the young at heart in my family,

and especially to Kaitlyn and Nathan,

my great-grandchildren,

and to those yet to be born.

Puddin

by
Pearl Bancroft

Chapter 1

My soft lumpy left leg was crossed over my soft lumpy right leg, and my listless arms hung at the sides of my new blue calico dress. There was silence all around. The family had gone to bed early, that is, all except Grandma. One string of popcorn drooped a little and touched my head. I sat leaning against a beautiful big box. There were packages all around me. Some were little and some were big, and they were all shapes. The moon smiled at me through the frosted window, but I wasn't smiling. I was afraid! And I was cold!

The farm house had been warm enough. And there had been happy excitement all day getting ready for Christmas. But something had chilled a

boy's heart, just like I felt, leaning against that big box. A doll was supposed to arrive in the last mail delivery for little Cathy. Her older brother Danny had opened the kitchen door. His Grandma saw the tears. There had been no doll in the mail box. His little sissy wanted a doll so much. He had shoveled snow three times for the neighbors, to earn enough money to order a doll out of the catalog. "Poor Sissy," he said sadly.

"Now don't you fret none," said Grandma. "Your Sissy will have her dolly." And after the others went to bed. Grandma turned on the light in the sewing room and pulled a bleached flour sack out of the bottom drawer of the chest. She snipped and sewed, and snipped and sewed. She stuffed me with pillow stuffing and made a beautiful dress out of

a blue calico print. It was while she sewed buttons on my dress, that she told me what happened that day. She said she didn't have time to put me in a box, so she tied a ribbon around my neck with a tag that read - love to Sissy, from Danny. Then she kissed me, looked up to the ceiling and said something like, "and thank you for your help," and put me under the tree.

The kiss felt good and made me feel warm inside until I started to wonder what the strangers upstairs were like. And even worse, what if Cathy would hate me for being here instead of a real doll?

I tried to go to sleep like people, but my eyes wouldn't close.So I just sat and worried, and the moon just kept smiling like he knew something I

didn't know. I must have been worrying terribly

hard, 'cause it seemed like no time at all and there

were lots of voices all at once shouting, "Merry

Christmas"! And the thumping down the stairs would

have hurt my ears if I had had them.

Grandma sat in the rocker, and Cathy and

Danny and their Mommy and Daddy sat on the floor.

Presents flew this way and that way. Somehow I got

pushed behind the tree. I didn't like it one bit! Was

this Christmas? Why were they so happy with all

this noise and mess?

When all the wrappings were cleared away,

I saw Danny nudge Grandma. She smiled and

reached behind the tree to rescue me from my

12

bewilderment. Danny's eyes lit up as he handed me to Cathy.

She looked a bit stunned at first. I was so scared! She turned me around, upside down, inspected my dress, and then she giggled and giggled, hugging me so hard, that some of my stuffing moved to different places. "I love you, I love you. You're the softest doll in the whole wide world. You're as soft as Grandma's plum puddin. I'll call you Puddin. Oh, Danny, she is my very favorite present of all!" Cathy nearly squeezed the stuffings out of me (but I didn't mind) while her Daddy read a story out of a big black book, which helped me to understand that Christmas was about a baby called Jesus . . . and Grandma looked very pleased.

Chapter II

Cathy kept me with her most all the time. After she dressed in the morning, she took hold of one of my arms and dragged me behind her. And away I went, plop, plop, plop down the stairs. She held on lovingly of course, which made all the difference in the world. Because she loved me so, is the reason I don't blame her for the time she left me in the woods. It rained, and my poor body got soaked clear through.

It was the middle of July, and Cathy's cousin Amy was staying on the farm for a short vacation. My, what fun they had riding the pony and picking wild flowers in the woods. Sometimes Grandma packed a lunch to take along.

16

Amy loved the woods and begged to go the last day of her vacation. But the sky was cloudy, and Grandma thought it best not to go. They were not allowed to go without a grown-up, so Grandma suggested that she make sugar cookies instead, and they could have cookies and lemonade on the porch.

Amy pouted. "It will spoil my whole vacation if I can't go to the woods my very last day."

Cathy didn't know what to do. She couldn't disobey her Grandma, but she couldn't let Amy go home disappointed either. Cathy's Mommy was doing errands in town, and Grandma had started to bake cookies. So Cathy thought, if they hurried, they could run to the woods real fast and play for

18

just a very little while. This would please Amy. Then they could run back in no time at all, before Grandma brought cookies to the porch. They would be sitting on the swing like good little girls, and this would please Grandma.

So off they went, Cathy dragging me behind as she always did. They picked flowers to their heart's content as if they had all the time in the world, when all of a sudden Cathy felt a rain drop. And then she remembered Grandma's cookies — "Oh dear, Grandma's cookies must be done — and it is going to rain. Hurry Amy!"

Away they ran and forgot all about me sitting against an old hickory tree, with my soft lumpy left leg crossed over my soft lumpy right leg, and my

listless arms hanging down the sides of my blue calico dress. I watched them running down the path between the trees till the path made a bend, and I couldn't see them anymore. The sky got very dark, and I heard a big crack in the sky, and the rain pushed through the tree and hit me hard! I got wet all through in no time.

But it didn't rain very long, and pretty soon the sky got light again. I was lonely and miserable sitting there all drippy wet. The birds began to sing again, which should have made me feel better. It didn't. I felt just plain awful! It seemed I was sitting there for hours feeling soggy and sad, when I looked down the path and saw Danny coming toward me.

"There you are Puddin. Sissy is crying her heart out", he said, as he picked me up and tried to squeeze the water out of me. "She thinks you are ruined and that she is being punished for disobeying Grandma."

When we got to the porch, we found that Cathy had sobbed herself to sleep on the swing. Grandma hurried me into the kitchen, wrung me out over the sink, then sat me in a chair in front of the open oven. Amy was no where in sight. She was probably packing, I thought. "Heat'en up the kitchen like this is crazy on a summer day, Puddin," said Grandma. "But I reckon this is an emergency."

I didn't know what she meant by emergency, but I felt better real fast and I was glad. I stayed in

the warm kitchen for a long time, then Grandma slipped upstairs with me and tucked me in Cathy's bed. I was still a little damp, but I figured she wanted to surprise Cathy, so it didn't matter. Now that I was warm and feeling myself once more, I forgave Cathy and hoped that they didn't scold her too much or punish her, because she was only trying to make everyone happy.

About the time I quit feeling sorry for me and started feeling sorry for Cathy, her Daddy carried her into the room and tucked her in bed. I didn't know what time it was 'cause the light was still peeking around the window shades.

When Cathy felt me next to her she woke up. Squealing for joy, she hugged me real tight and promised Jesus, (I guess it was the same one who was born on Christmas) that she would never disobey again or leave me outside in the rain. And she said she loved him and she loved me . . . and I thought, it really didn't matter that I had still been a little damp 'cause her tears dampened me some more.

Chapter III

It was Sunday. Cathy held me in her arms all the way down stairs, instead of letting me go plop, plop, plop behind her as usual. She was very quiet at breakfast, but said please and thank you at the right times.

It took longer for her to eat that morning, for she would not put me down for a minute. And when the family was about to leave for Sunday School, she begged her Mommy to let me go too.

When Cathy's friends saw me, they giggled. Small chairs formed a circle and children filled up every one except one. Then a pretty lady came

29

and sat there. "Why don't you introduce your friend, Cathy?" she asked. So Cathy did.

The pretty lady talked for a long time about how much Jesus loved children and how much He wanted them to love Him too. And if they did, they would obey their parents. When she said that, Cathy squeezed me hard.

After the pretty lady said good-by to the children and gave Cathy and me a hug all at the same time, we went up some stairs and sat next to Grandma in a great big beautiful room with a window like I'd never seen before. Lots of people sat on the same long seat together. I wondered where they all came from. Then some people sang a very nice song. They had long bath robes

on. Cathy's Mommy was singing with them, but

her robe was not the same one she usually wore

at night when she tucked Cathy into bed. It was

shiny and silky and black. Cathy put me on the seat

beside her, and I sat with my soft lumpy left leg

crossed over my soft lumpy right leg, and my

listless arms hung at the sides of my blue calico

dress. I couldn't understand the man behind the big

box in front of the room. I kept looking at that

beautiful window, all bright colors like Grandma's

cotton scraps in her sewing basket. The sun was

shining through so brightly that I felt I was sitting

in the sunshine with all the children in the window.

They were sitting all around a man who was

holding a very small child on his lap. I wondered if it

was a picture of Jesus, 'cause the pretty lady said

He loved children. He must love Cathy. I had a hard

time understanding people things, but I knew that
love meant being kind and hugging and
wanting someone more than anything else, 'cause
that is how it was when Cathy said she loved me.

Then the man behind the box said
something about God's blessing on us all, and
people started to leave the big room. I wanted to
stay and look at the beautiful picture window, but
Grandma gave Cathy a nudge, which meant we had
to go. I couldn't forget how kind Jesus looked, and I
was glad that Cathy talked to Him every night when
she snuggled up to me.

36

Chapter IV

The school bus didn't come. It was dark even though it was morning. Everyone was sitting around the big table for breakfast a little later than usual. Cathy was big enough to sit on a grown-up chair, so she put me on her stool. It was close to the stove. I was glad to be there, 'cause it was so warm.

"No one can go outside today," said Cathy's Daddy. The wind was making an awful noise and snow was whirling against the windows. Pepper, the dog, was even allowed to be in the kitchen to keep warm. He usually had to stay outside so he could run around.

Cathy's Daddy had talked to God before breakfast. I couldn't understand why he talked to

God and Cathy talked to Jesus. I knew Jesus was born at Christmas and when He grew up He loved children, but who was God?

Well, we sat a long time at the table. Cathy's Daddy started to read out of his big black book again. Grandma smiled a contented smile, but Cathy's Mommy kept looking out the window. I didn't understand a lot of the words, but Cathy's Daddy said that Jesus was saying the words he was reading.

Cathy and Danny were drinking hot chocolate while they were listening. It looked so good. Grandma had put a little soft cloud of something on top, and I wished I had a real tummy.

40

Pepper snuggled on the rug. Then I listened again to Cathy's Daddy read. I heard him say God, then some other words, then, "it is my father . . . He is your God." Hmm! Guess Cathy's Daddy talks to the father of Jesus, and His name is God.

Then the telephone rang. Pepper barked, and Grandma poured more coffee in the grownups cups. Cathy's Daddy said that he would answer the phone, but Cathy said that she wanted to. Her Daddy told her to stay at the table and finish drinking her hot chocolate. "No, I want to," she insisted. She jumped up and darted from the table, spilling her hot chocolate all over. Some even got on my dress. When her Daddy picked up the phone, she pouted!

Grandma started to wipe up the mess, and

Cathy's Mommy took hold of Cathy's hand and they went to Grandma's sewing room. I don't know what they were doing, but they were gone a long time. When they came back, Cathy told her Daddy she was sorry she didn't obey and thanked Grandma for washing out the spots on my dress. Her Daddy gave her a hug and said he loved her, and Grandma hugged her too, and said, "I reckon we are going to have a happy day." And they did.

While the wind howled, they played games on the table, and laughed. The snow kept whirling against the windows, and I was sitting with my soft lumpy left leg crossed over my soft lumpy right leg, and my listless arms hung at the sides of my damp blue calico dress, and Pepper was still on the rug in front of the stove, wagging his tail.

Chapter V

One morning Cathy kissed me and sat me lovingly in her little oak rocking chair, in front of the corner windows in her room. She didn't hold my hand and go plop, plop, plop down the stairs. I heard every step she made down, down, down, and I sort of twisted up inside.

I knew that Cathy was growing up and I was feeling sad, 'cause I didn't get hugged as much anymore, or dragged here and there where things were going on. I was lonely. I sat watching the ruffles on the curtain move just a little now and then when a breeze came through the open windows.

It seemed I sat for hours, but I know it really wasn't, when I heard Grandma coming up the

stairs. I knew it was her 'cause she stepped softly. She quietly came into Cathy's room, picked me up, gave me a very hard squeeze, which I loved, moved slowly down the stairs to her sewing room, me in her arms, and didn't say a word the whole time.

She coughed a couple times while she sewed the buttons tighter on my dress that were loose. And she mended my feet that were worn from Cathy going plop, plop, plop down the stairs with me. She hugged me again and fell asleep in her chair, with me in her arms.

The school bus honked its horn for Cathy and Danny long ago, and Cathy's Mommy was cleaning the house. I could always tell 'cause she sang happy songs, and hurried upstairs and downstairs,

and sometimes turned on the record player and sang even louder. Otherwise she didn't sing at all like that, except in church when she wore that black robe.

She finally came in the sewing room with a dust cloth in her hand, singing something about the "arms of Jesus." Then she saw Grandma sleeping in the chair. She stopped singing. "Grandma", she said softly. "Grandma." Putting her arms around her, she hugged her, I fell on the floor, and she began to sob. "Oh Grandma, you really are, you really are in His arms!" She ran to the phone in the kitchen and talked to somebody, then came back and cried again and said, "You must be so happy. I'm so glad you are so happy with Jesus." I didn't understand why she was crying. Grandma was just sleeping.

Then Cathy's Mommy picked me up and said, "You are part of Grandma's love to us. You are very special, Puddin." She carried me to the kitchen and sat me on the high stool. There I sat for a long time with my soft lumpy left leg crossed over my soft lumpy right leg and my listless arms hung at the sides of my blue calico dress.

Lots of strange people came to visit. It wasn't even lunch time yet when Cathy's Daddy came in the kitchen door with Cathy and Danny. Cathy saw me on the stool and grabbed me so fast, hugging me, and cried 'til I felt damp. Danny put his arm around her and said, "Don't cry Sissy. We should all be happy. Grandma is in the beautiful house Jesus has in Heaven, and she can be with Grandpa, and Jesus will take good care of her, even better than

we could." "Really, Danny, she really is happy?"
"She really is," said Danny.

Cathy hung on to me real tight, it felt so
good again, and ran upstairs to her room, and like
she was all tired out, fell asleep on her bed while
she clung to me. I don't know what was going on
downstairs. I just couldn't understand how everyone
was so sad, when they said they were so happy.
. . . Then I thought if Heaven is anything like that
beautiful window at church, where Jesus is loving
the children so tenderly, then I guess Grandma will
be very happy!

Chapter VI

For a long time Cathy kept me on her bed with two little patchwork pillows. The colors were bright in the pillows, but my dress was really faded. I still got hugged every morning when she made her bed. Then she'd prop me up again by those pretty pillows. It was almost like she was a little girl again, except that she had packed all of her other toys in a big trunk and pushed it way back in her closet.

I felt special to still be a part of her life and was content by the pillows 'til Amy came to visit again. This time it was to celebrate Cathy's sixteenth birthday . . . and I got put back in the rocking chair. But I didn't mind, 'cause Amy was such a giggling,

happy girl. It seemed the whole house laughed when she was there.

The first night the girls came upstairs late, and they talked 'til it was almost light outside. Amy teased Cathy about the time she left me in the woods in the rain. It made Cathy cry 'cause it reminded her of Grandma. She missed her so. Then she picked me up and gave me a hug and said, "But I still have you Puddin."

In the morning there was a lot of commotion down stairs. Amy had gone off to school with Cathy, and Cathy's Mom was cleaning with the vacuum, moving things and singing. There was to be a big birthday party that night. Every year there was a party for Danny and one for Cathy, and a big cake was put in the center of the table with flowers and

candles on it. Everyone would say how good it was. I don't understand about food, but it seemed too bad to cut up something so pretty into little pieces.

Suddenly, I heard Cathy's Mom come up the stairs. She came in Cathy's room and picked me up, and downstairs we went. Instead of putting the cake in the center of the dining room table, she sat me there and tied the string of a balloon on each of my wrists. One pink and one blue. That was great for me 'cause I could see everything that was going on.

Later in the day, Cathy and Amy came home from school, slamming the kitchen door. Cathy ran into the dining room, throwing jacket and books on

a chair. "Oh Mom. I love the table! And Puddin looks so cute holding those balloons."

When it started to get dark outside, people began to arrive.

When Cathy was a little girl, her parties were on Saturday, but now that she was more grown up, they were in the evening.

My, what noise and laughing. (Danny wasn't there 'cause he was away at college, and wouldn't be home 'til Christmas.) They played games and Cathy opened presents. Then came time to have the birthday cake.

Cathy's Daddy said they would have the

blessing first. He thanked God for giving Cathy to them and said how wonderful it was to know that Cathy had believed in Jesus when she was a little girl, so she could one day be in Heaven. He said, "Jesus, help her to walk with you."

I didn't understand the walking part, but I had it straight now that God was the Father and He sent His son, Jesus, down from Heaven to love people and to die like Grandma, only He came alive again. I heard Cathy's Daddy say once that Jesus was punished for all the bad things people do, which is called sin. God can't have sin in Heaven, so Jesus was punished for people, so God could let them be in Heaven. But people have to believe this with their hearts. Then they can go there.

After everyone left the party, Cathy picked me up and said, "Puddin, you are still my very favorite present." Then she carried me upstairs and cuddled me in bed that night, like she did when she was a little girl, even though Amy was there. It wasn't long before my arm was a little damp.

Chapter VII

It was so lonesome in the house when Cathy went to college. I sat in the little oak rocker all the time, but the rocker was in a new place now. Cathy's Mom said one day, "It's far too lonesome for me with the children off to school. I think your rocker should be in the kitchen, Puddin, so we can keep each other company," And so it was. And it did help. That is, for a while it helped. Then Cathy's Mom got a letter from her. "Oh! Mom," it said, "I miss home so much. Do you suppose you and Daddy could bring my little rocker when you come to visit? It would make it a little like home. Of course Puddin must come too. My friends would love her."

68

And so they did. Take me to school with the rocker, I mean, and her friends did love me. I hadn't had so much attention since my first Christmas. They all hugged me lots, and when they had problems, they talked to me about them and when they didn't feel good, they talked to me about it, and when they were just talking to each other, they talked to me.

They were so silly some times about their clothes. When they were going out at night, they would try on their clothes, then each other's clothes. It made me tired just to watch them. All the time I was sitting in the rocker, with my soft lumpy left leg crossed over my soft lumpy right leg and my listless arms hung at the sides of the same blue calico dress.

One night Cathy got all dressed up in a long dress, and her hair was piled on top of her head in big curls. She looked so pretty. It was a very special night. She was going to a party with someone very special.

She picked me up and hugged me so tight, I thought the stuffing might pop out some of my old seams. "I'm so in love, Puddin. Wait 'til you see my Mr. Cassidy. You'll love him too." She put me down, looked in the mirror once more and hurried away.

I wasn't sure about this Mr. Cassidy business . . . then Cathy's roommate came in with piles of books, plugged in the coffee pot, gave me a hug, and said we were in for a long night.

So, I sat in the rocking chair staring at all those books, and knew I wasn't going to like Mr. Cassidy.

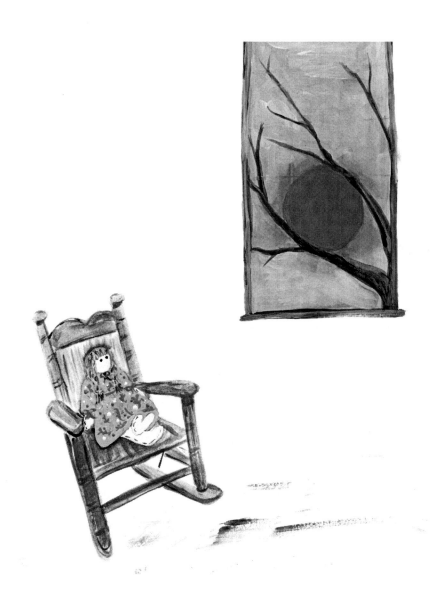

Chapter VIII

I sat in the rocker with my left leg crossed over my right leg as usual, with my listless arms hung at the sides of my faded blue calico dress, looking out the window of the second story dorm. The sun was setting and it looked just like a ball of fire. It looked like it was perched for a while on a tree limb, then it dropped and I couldn't see it anymore.

Cathy was sewing on a skirt. She mumbled to herself a lot. I don't know why she didn't talk to me instead, 'cause I'd been sort of lonely with her gone so much from her room.

All of a sudden there was a knock on her door and lots of girls pushed into the room and yelled something about being late — the bus was waiting — and the boys were impatient.

Up Jumped Cathy with the skirt in her hand, and said, "Everything happens at once. Oh boy, I'll never finish in time. Come on Puddin, I'll take you along for good luck."

I was swished into the air and landed in the arms of one of her friends, who hopped into the bus just before it started moving.

What a noise there was! Only a few girls were there. The rest were boys. Two boys started tossing a ball back and forth.

Cathy kept sewing on her skirt. The other girls were wearing skirts like the one she was sewing. Guess she was supposed to have hers on too, but it wasn't ready yet.

Then one of the boys looked at me, picked me up and said, "What are you doing on the players' bus?"

"She's going to bring you good luck, Mike," replied Cathy. "You guys sure need it this year." He sort of grinned and tossed me back to the seat behind him. I landed on top of Cathy's skirt and almost got stitched to it.

After the bus stopped, the girls went into a building in a room like a big bathroom without bath

79

tubs. There were other girls in there giggling and talking, and they had their skirts on alike too, but not like Cathy's. Cathy slipped her's on and fixed herself in a big hurry. Then she and her friends took me and went into a huge room where boys were bouncing balls and it was as noisy as the bus had been.

Cathy perched me on sort of a bench and ran out on the floor to jump and yell with the other girls. I didn't understand what they were doing, but they seemed to really like it, and they did somersaults, and cartwheels and other tricky things. Then they sat on the bench beside me.

A bunch of boys gathered in a tight circle at one end of the big room, and another bunch at the other end. It looked like they were talking to Jesus 'cause they bowed their heads for a little bit. Then

they all yelled and started running back and forth on the floor, until a man with black stripes blew a whistle. Then they stopped.

They must have been so tired running like that. Once in a while, the girls would hurry to the floor and yell and do their tricks. Sometimes they would sit down, then each one would squeeze me and say, "You're making it work, Puddin." Making what work? I wasn't doing anything, and I couldn't understand very well what they were doing either.

Then, there was a big whistle, and all Cathy's friends around yelled and jumped up and down, and Cathy hugged me again and said she was glad she brought me. I think I was glad too, 'cause I got so many hugs. It was much better than sitting alone in the rocking chair.

83

The boy they called Mike came over to Cathy and said, "We did it!" She replied, "I told you Puddin would bring us luck." "I think you are a bit confused, Cathy", he said.

When we got back on the bus, the loud noise turned to singing, and it reminded me of what it sounded like those few times when Cathy took me to church. Then I thought again about the lady in Cathy's class, and how she talked about Jesus and how He loved children and said they should talk to Him. And I thought about how the boys bowed their heads, like they were talking to Jesus. And Mike said Cathy was confused about me bringing them luck. Mike must have meant that Jesus helped them win.

That night before Cathy climbed into bed, she hugged me and talked to Jesus, like she did when she was a little girl. She wasn't confused!

Chapter IX

It seemed so warm and cozy back in Cathy's home again. She was through with college. I was sitting in the rocking chair in the living room by the fireplace. My soft lumpy left leg crossed over my soft lumpy right leg, and my listless arms hung at the sides of my faded blue calico dress.

Strange people had been going in and out all day long and no one even noticed me. Pepper barked a lot outside. I didn't know what was going on.

Then the man who was behind the big box in church, that time when I went to church with Cathy,

89

sat in the big chair. Cathy and Mr. Cassidy sat close on the sofa. I didn't like that very much.

The man talked to them about getting married, whatever that meant. He said he was glad they both trusted in Jesus, that God should be the center of their home, and a lot of things I just didn't understand. Why was he there anyway?

Then they had coffee — he said "good-bye" and he would see them on Saturday.

What was happening on Saturday? Well, when Saturday came, there was a big breakfast and lots of noise from the kitchen. Then everyone got all dressed up. Cathy looked beautiful in a long white shiny dress. Even Danny had on a suit, and it wasn't even Sunday.

All at once, the house was empty, except for Pepper and me. They let him come in the kitchen. But after they left, he seemed to feel sad too. I could hear him cry. He crept into the living room, looked up at me, licked my right foot and lay down by my chair and went to sleep. . . . Then I didn't feel so lonely.

94

Chapter X

My soft lumpy left leg was crossed over my soft lumpy right leg, and my listless arms hung at the sides of my faded blue calico print dress. I sat this way in the Cassidy's family room for six years, in the little oak rocking chair. That is, I was in that position most of the time. Cathy dusted twice a week. So twice a week I got picked up and squeezed, and then was put back in that very same position again. Once in a while Cathy picked me up and hugged me for no reason at all and said, "I still love you, Puddin."

Mr. Cassidy didn't pay much attention to me. He smiled at me sometimes when Cathy wasn't looking, but I was never sure if he really liked me.

96

I knew he didn't love me, 'cause loving meant hugging, and when Cathy hugged me, it made me so happy. I would feel all warm inside.

Well, it wouldn't have been so bad sitting in the rocker, getting hugged twice a week, but something happened at the Cassidy's to make my poor cotton insides all twist up. The Cassidy's were going to have a baby. Maybe I wouldn't get hugged anymore, or maybe I couldn't sit in the little oak rocking chair anymore. Oh my!

On the day Mr. Cassidy was to bring Cathy home from the hospital, he carried the rocking chair into a little room with blue walls. Then he picked me up and said, "What are we going to do with you?

Little boys don't like dolls." Then he put me down.

Oh my! Oh my! What is going to happen to me, I wondered? Mr. Cassidy shut the door of the little room. I felt so bad inside. Maybe Cathy wouldn't dust in this strange room and I would never be hugged again. I sat a long time with my soft lumpy left leg crossed over my soft lumpy right leg and my listless arms hung at the sides of my faded blue calico dress, and watched the door.

Then I heard Cathy and Mr. Cassidy laugh and the door opened. Cathy was holding a soft white blanket with both arms. She looked so happy and giggled, just like that Christmas when she found me under the Christmas tree. Mr. Cassidy

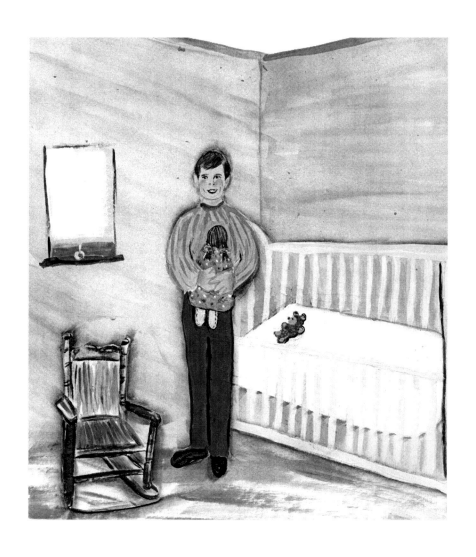

100

took the blanket as Cathy lifted the new baby out of it. She stepped toward the little bed to lay the baby down, when she tripped on the rocking chair. The baby slid from her arms on to my soft lumpy legs. Cathy gasped! Mr. Cassidy let the blanket fall to the floor to grab the baby, but he was safe on my lap.

"Oh Jamie, Jamie, I didn't see the rocking chair." Cathy picked up the baby, as the tears choked up in her throat from sudden fright. She held him close to her.

Mr. Cassidy stooped down, took me from the rocking chair, hugged me, and said, "Puddin, I love you"!

Chapter XI

The sunlight peaked around the edges of the window shade. Jamie was still sleeping. He looked so cute sleeping on his tummy, with his knees tucked under it, and his little plump bottom was pushed up like a little mountain. His head was hiding under his bear and his tiny fist was tight around one corner of a soft flannel quilt.

I remember when Cathy made that quilt. She sat in the family room, curled up in a big tufted chair by the fireplace. Every time she picked up the sewing basket, filled with pretty soft flannel pieces, she talked to Jesus just like He was right in the room with us. She said He was so good to give

Mr. Cassidy and her a miracle. Her face was so shiny bright! But I didn't know what she meant by miracle. She couldn't mean the quilt, 'cause she was making that herself.

When she picked up the basket one day, she said, "I love you Jesus for giving us this baby." I thought. Could a baby be a miracle? I thought, and I thought, and I thought.

I thought about how I was made. I remembered again how Grandma made me. She sewed me, stuffed me, and dressed me — and there I was! But I didn't understand how to make a baby. It seemed like Cathy and Jesus had a secret. And she kept thanking Him, like maybe He was making the baby. She had to wait a very long time. Jesus

WAS making the baby — THAT was the miracle!
How wonderful He must be, and smarter even than
Grandma to make a real baby. A miracle must be
something only Jesus can do.

Jamie woke up and stretched his little arms
and legs, and he wriggled out from under his bear.
His little eyes studied the quilt, and for some time
was amused by the sun's rays dancing on the walls.
Then he turned his head and saw me sitting in the
rocker staring at him with my soft lumpy left leg
crossed over my soft lumpy right leg, and my
listless arms hung at the sides of my faded blue
calico dress . . . and he giggled!

Printed in the United States
119202LV00007B/124-162/P